Five reasons why you'll fall in love with Nixie!

Bumblebees' Bottoms! Nixie's always getting in trouble!

A completely new kind of fairy in Fairyland.

Rainbow Fairies meets Horrid Henry!

Full of magical mishaps and ingenious inventions!

A wonderfully funny story, packed with gorgeous illustrations.

We love Nixie!

'She's like Horrid Henry with wings!'
Wondrous Reads

'The lovely and lovable Nixie continues to cast her special spell on all those fairy-loving, adventure-seeking youngsters who know that being good all the time is just pure fiction!'
Pam Norfolk, The Star

'Here's one fab fairy: she has bucketloads of cheek and attitude.'
Jill Bennet, Red Reading Hub

'With her clompy boots, holey tights and a wonky wand, you know that Nixie is not going to be like any other fairy you will have met before.'
Book Lover Jo

Getting to know Nixie!

Nixie, the Bad, Bad Fairy is the most mischievous fairy in the whole of Fairyland, but most of the time it's her wonky wand that's to blame!

Here's a list of her biggest ever blunders:

- TURNING THE FAIRY GODMOTHER INTO A CUPCAKE WITH A SWIRL OF BUTTER ICING ON HER HEAD AND A CHERRY ON TOP
- CRACKING THE TURRET OF THE ROYAL PALACE IN HALF WITH A BOLT OF LIGHTNING FROM HER WONKY WAND
- TURNING THE ROYAL COACH INTO A BUBBLE WHICH BLEW AWAY—WITH THE FAIRY QUEEN STILL INSIDE
- CAUSING A BLIZZARD—INSIDE THE FAIRY GODMOTHER'S KITCHEN
- ENCHANTING HER BIG RED CLOMPY BOOTS TO DANCE . . . SO THEY DANCED ACROSS A TABLE UP THE WALL AND ONTO THE CEILING—WITH HER INSIDE THEM HANGING UPSIDE DOWN

For Gaia, I'm having the most magical time. Thanks to you - Cas

For Charlie Berthon - Ali

OXFORD
UNIVERSITY PRESS

Great Clarendon Street, Oxford OX2 6DP

Oxford University Press is a department of the University of Oxford. It furthers the University's objective of excellence in research, scholarship, and education by publishing worldwide. Oxford is a registered trademark of Oxford University Press in the UK and in certain other countries

First published 2016

British Library Cataloguing in Publication Data

Data available

ISBN: 978-0-19-274487-6

1 3 5 7 9 10 8 6 4 2

Printed in Great Britain

Paper used in the production of this book is a natural, recyclable product made from wood grown in sustainable forests. The manufacturing process conforms to the environmental regulations of the country of origin.

Nixie

Fizzy Firework Fun

Cas Lester

Illustrated by Ali Pye

OXFORD
UNIVERSITY PRESS

Contents

Chapter 1

PRIZES

THWACK!

A little wooden ball smacked into a hazelnut and knocked it to the ground.

'Yahoo!' cried Nixie the Bad, Bad Fairy. She'd scored a hit with her very first throw! Her little black wings fluttered excitedly against her grubby red dress. She picked

up a second ball, screwed one eye shut, took aim and hurled the ball at another target on the hazelnut shy.

SMACK!

'Woohoo!' she cried, as another nut toppled to the ground.

'One more hit and you'll win a prize!' said the Palace Fairy who was running the shy.

Nixie's friends, Fizz the Wish Fairy, Fidget the Butterfly Fairy, and Twist the Cobweb Fairy, all crossed their fingers for luck.

It was long after dark, and way after bedtime, but all the fairies were at the Fairyland Funfair and Fireworks night!

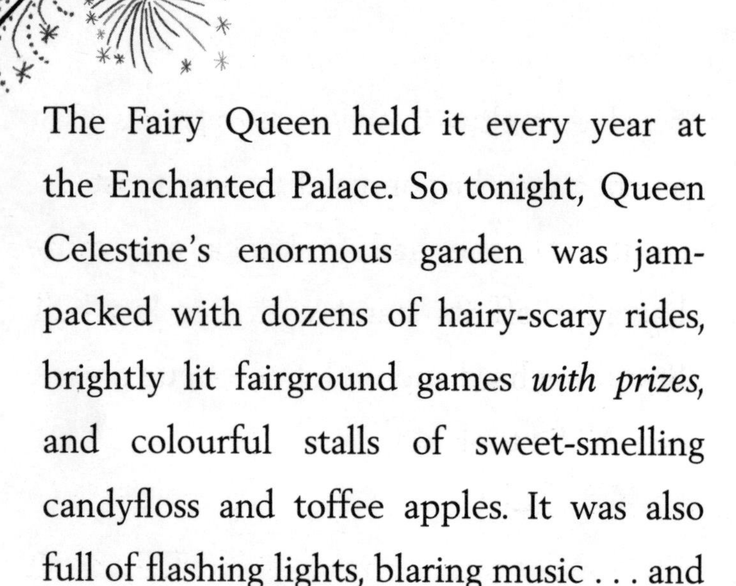

The Fairy Queen held it every year at the Enchanted Palace. So tonight, Queen Celestine's enormous garden was jam-packed with dozens of hairy-scary rides, brightly lit fairground games *with prizes*, and colourful stalls of sweet-smelling candyfloss and toffee apples. It was also full of flashing lights, blaring music . . . and noisy fairies! All laughing and screaming and yelling their heads off!

Nixie loved the fair—especially the dodgems, the spinning teacups, and the helter-skelter. But first of all tonight, she'd rushed over to the hazelnut shy, to make sure she had the pick of the prizes! She couldn't decide between a giant blow-up

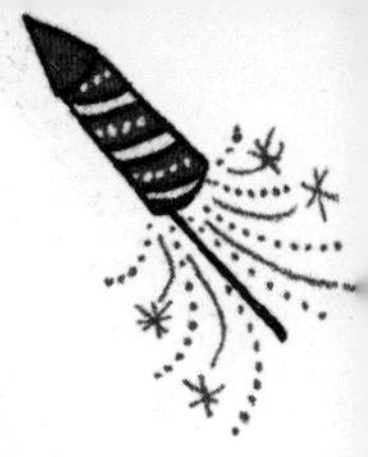

hammer, a glow-in-the-dark water pistol or an enormous bag of marshmallow twists . . .

But first, she had to knock one more hazelnut off its stand with her last ball. Squinting hard and with her tongue poking out, Nixie took aim.

CRACK!

She hit the nut . . . but it didn't fall off! It did a mighty wobble and Nixie held her breath as . . . tremble, topple, teeter . . .

PLONK!

'YES!' whooped Nixie as the nut finally fell off. Now to pick her prize. It was hard to make up her mind but eventually she chose the marshmallows. She ripped open the bag, shoved a couple into her mouth

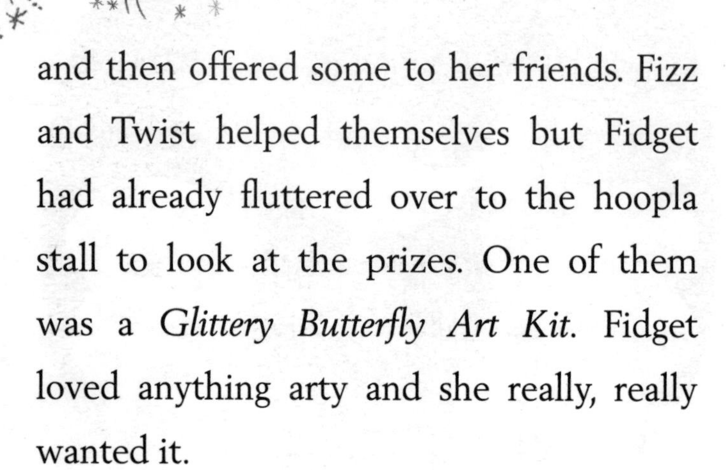

and then offered some to her friends. Fizz and Twist helped themselves but Fidget had already fluttered over to the hoopla stall to look at the prizes. One of them was a *Glittery Butterfly Art Kit*. Fidget loved anything arty and she really, really wanted it.

'Fidget!' called Nixie. But Fidget didn't answer. So Nixie called louder, 'FIDGET!' And then even louder, 'FIDGET!'

But Fidget couldn't hear her—partly because the fair was so noisy, but mostly because Fidget was wearing a pair of *huge* fluffy earmuffs.

Nixie fluttered over and tapped her on the shoulder.

'Take them off!' she yelled. 'It isn't even that cold.'

'I'm not wearing them because I'm cold,' laughed Fidget, slipping the earmuffs off. 'It's because I don't like the noise of the fireworks.'

'But the fireworks won't be for ages yet,' pointed out Nixie and held out the sweet bag to her. So Fidget left her earmuffs round her

neck and took a handful of marshmallows.

'What shall we do next?' asked Nixie, fizzing with excitement. There were so many rides and stalls!

Fizz wanted a go on the hazelnut shy, but Fidget said she'd rather go on the hoopla, and Twist wanted a toffee apple.

'How about the dodgems!' cried Nixie. And without waiting for an answer she grabbed Twist and Fidget and hauled them through the crowds of fairies.

'What about my go on the hazelnut shy!' cried Fizz.

'You can do that later! Come on!' yelled Nixie over her shoulder.

So Fizz darted after her.

Chapter 2

YAHOO! DODGEMS!

VROOOM . . .

Dodgem cars roared madly round the track as Nixie and the others dashed up to the ride. The fairies driving the cars were laughing and squealing and bashing into each other like crazy!

BUMP! BONK!

It looked brilliant fun and Nixie waited impatiently for the ride to stop. Lots of other fairies were already hovering around the track all wanting a go, and she was worried she might not get a car. As soon as the ride had stopped there was a mad scramble. Nixie **charged** onto the track and jumped into a car, grabbing the one next to it for Fizz.

'FIZZ!' she called.

But just as Fizz reached the dodgem, Adorabella the Goody-goody Fairy leapt into it!

'Hey! I was saving that for Fizz,' snapped Nixie.

'Well I got it first,' replied Adorabella,

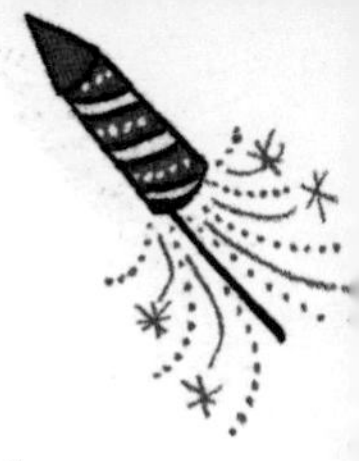

smoothing her frilly yellow fairy dress smugly.

'Get out!' ordered Nixie.

'No!' retorted Adorabella, gripping onto the wheel.

Nixie seethed, her green eyes glittering dangerously. She looked around for another car for Fizz, but by now they were all full.

'Never mind, I'll have a go next time,' he shrugged.

'No! Come in mine,' cried Nixie, budging over on the seat. 'But I'm driving!'

Fizz grinned and clambered in beside her.

As soon as the ride started, Nixie pushed the 'go' pedal flat to the floor with her big red clompy boot and the car hurtled off

around the track!

VAROOOM!

'YAHOO!' yelled Nixie. Fizz whooped and held on tight!

Fidget and Twist were sharing a dodgem car too. But Fidget couldn't get the hang of the steering and they were weaving around all over the track!

'Look out!' squealed Twist . . . and they bashed into Nixie's car with a huge

BUMP!

They all burst out laughing, then Nixie drove off, heading straight for another car—it was Adorabella's.

VROOOM . . . BASH!

'Gotcha!' cried Nixie gleefully.

'You did that on purpose!' squealed Adorabella.

'Of course I did!' grinned Nixie wickedly.

'That's what you're supposed to do on the dodgems!' laughed Fizz.

'Well, don't do it again!' glared Adorabella trying to drive away, but Nixie chased after her, and soon . . .

BONK!

She bumped Adorabella's car again!

'Stop picking on me!' wailed Adorabella.

'Serves you right for pinching Fizz's car!' yelled Nixie.

'I'm telling the Fairy Godmother on you!' retorted Adorabella.

And, as soon as the ride stopped,

Adorabella stormed off to tell tales. But Tabitha Quicksilver, the Fairy Godmother, was waiting in the queue on the steps of the **helter-skelter** with the Fairy Queen. Adorabella tried shouting up to her, but the fair was too noisy and she couldn't make the Fairy Godmother hear her. So she clenched her fists and fumed, and thought about how to get Nixie back.

Meanwhile, Nixie and her friends were working out what to do next.

'The spinning teacups!' cried Nixie, her eyes shining with excitement.

But Twist said she didn't like them. Fidget wanted to go on the **hoopla** stall to try to win the *Glittery Butterfly Art Kit* before

anyone else did, and Fizz pointed out he still hadn't had a go at the **hazelnut shy.**

'But we have to go on the teacups—they make you go all **super dizzy,'** insisted Nixie. 'COME ON!' she yelled, dashing off.

Fidget sighed, and Fizz and Twist rolled their eyes, but they all fluttered after Nixie.

Chapter 3

BOSSY BRITCHES

Nixie had already bagsied a teacup by the time the others caught up with her. Fizz and Fidget clambered in next to her but Twist hung back.

'Hurry up, Twist!' called Nixie.

Twist shook her head. 'I'm not coming on.'

'Don't be silly,' said Nixie and she grabbed Twist's arm and tried to pull her into the giant cup.

'I don't want to,' cried Twist. 'The spinning makes me feel sick.'

'She doesn't have to come on if she doesn't want to,' said Fizz.

'Stop being so **bossy,** Nixie,' added Fidget.

'I'm not!' said Nixie hotly, her little face going as red as her dress. 'I'm just trying to make sure everybody's having fun, that's all.'

'But I don't think it *is* fun,' said Twist.

'Fine!' snapped Nixie. 'But I don't think it'll be much fun sitting there all on your own while we're on the ride!'

Fidget didn't think so either, so she stood up to get out of the teacup.

'Come on, Twist, we can go and do the hoopla instead,' she said.

'Noooo!' cried Nixie, grabbing hold of her. But then the music started and the ride began to move. Fidget had no choice but to stay on.

'We won't be long!' Nixie promised Twist.

Twist sat on the grass, hugging her knees and watching her friends. They were having a brilliant time, **whirling** round

and round in their teacup and squealing excitedly every time it span super fast. But the ride went on for *ages.* Twist sighed and looked around at the rest of the fair. Everyone else was having loads of fun. She was the only one on her own. Willow the Tree Fairy and some Woodland Fairies were whizzing down the helter-skelter. The Winter Fairies were all on the big wheel. And Adorabella was on the merry-go-round with Briar the Flower Fairy and Dulcie the Tooth Fairy, *and* they were munching toffee apples.

Maybe I could go off and get a toffee apple, thought Twist. But what if the teacup ride ended while she was gone?

The others wouldn't know where she was. She sighed and hoped the ride would end soon.

As she was waiting, Twist could see the Fairy Queen and the Fairy Godmother having a go at the hook-a-duck game. The Fairy Godmother was hopeless at it but Queen Celestine won a pair of **fake glasses** with a **false nose** and **moustache.** She tried them on and The Fairy Godmother burst out laughing.

Twist giggled—the beautiful Fairy Queen looked utterly ridiculous.

Eventually, the spinning teacups slowed to a stop and Fizz, Fidget, and Nixie got off and staggered giddily over to Twist. They looked so funny trying to walk in a straight line, but zigzagging wildly and tripping over each other! Twist laughed out loud.

'Twist! Help! I'm all dizzy!' squealed Nixie. So Twist jumped up and Nixie grabbed hold of her and they both giggled. 'What shall we do now?' gasped Nixie.

'I think Twist should choose,' announced Fidget.

'That's only fair,' agreed Fizz.

'So what are we going to do, Twist?'

asked Nixie jumping up and down, her little wings **fizzing** in excitement.

'The ladybird ride!' cried Twist.

'Ooooh, yes!' squeaked Nixie, but just then, the sweet tempting smell of candyfloss drifted across from the brightly-lit sweet stall and up her fairy nose. 'I know! Let's get some candyfloss first!' she cried.

'I'd rather have a toffee apple,' said Twist.

'Me too,' said Fizz

'But the toffee apple stall is *miles* away on the other side of the fair!' wailed Nixie. 'And the candyfloss is just over here!' And she darted over to the stall, pulling Twist with her.

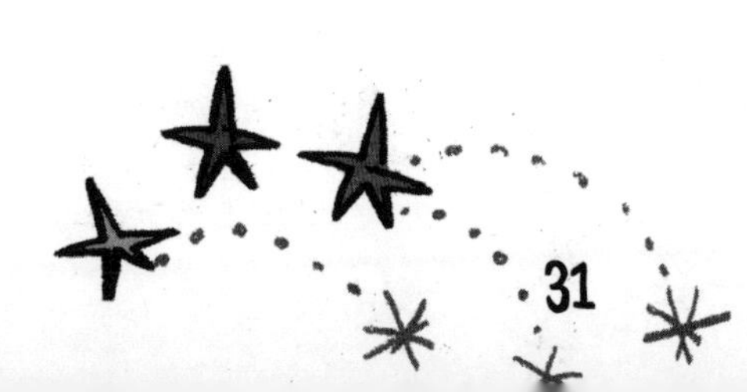

Chapter 4

BUZBY'S CANDYFLOSS DISASTER!

Buzby, the Fairy Godmother's little honeybee assistant, was running the candyfloss stall. Well that's what he was meant to be doing. But he was having a bit of bother getting the swirls of sticky pink sugar to stay on the sticks. A group of fairies were clustered around him waiting

for their candyfloss, so Nixie and her friends joined them.

Buzby was getting very flustered—and very sticky! His little wings fluttered anxiously as he hovered above the spinning bowl, trying to catch the whirling sugar strands. But every time he managed to get a small blob of candyfloss on to a stick, it suddenly went lopsided and whizzed off! Dollops of pink fluffy candyfloss flew out of the bowl! Whoops! The fairies thought it was hilarious! Giggling excitedly, they darted about catching the flying clumps and stuffing them in their mouths!

Nixie and her friends were quick to join in the fun. A particularly large lump suddenly

whizzed off over their heads. Tensing her little wings, Nixie shot upwards to catch it.

'Got it!' she cried, then tore it into bits, to share with the others. It was a bit gooey by the time she'd handed it around, but it was still **sugary** and **prickly** on their tongues.

By now poor Buzby was very frustrated—and plastered with candyfloss! He picked up a new stick, leant over the bowl, and tried again, waggling his antennae in concentration. But, to his horror, the sticky strands of sugar suddenly caught on his antennae and wound round and round them! He looked like he was wearing a pair of fluffy pink candyfloss pom-poms! The fairies tried very hard not to giggle.

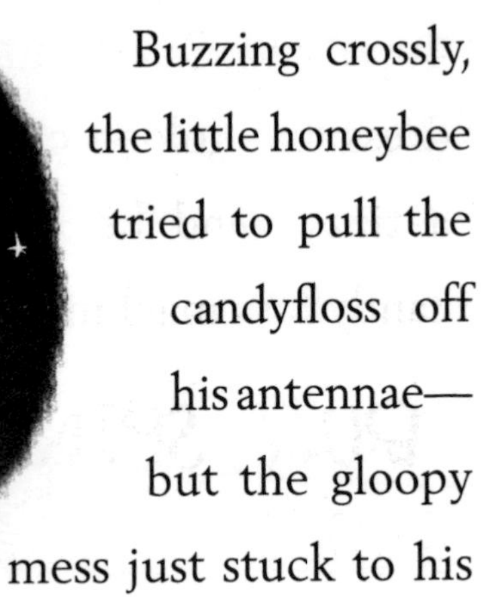

Buzzing crossly, the little honeybee tried to pull the candyfloss off his antennae—but the gloopy mess just stuck to his arms instead. And the more he tried to unstick himself—the more tangled up and covered in candyfloss he became.

Buzby had almost managed to untangle his wings from a particularly sticky clump when the Fairy Queen and the Fairy Godmother arrived. Queen Celestine was telling the little honeybee how much she *loved* candyfloss, but the sight of

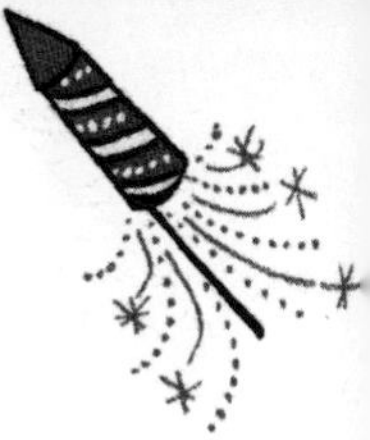

the Fairy Queen in her beautiful long dress and golden crown put Buzby all in a tizzy—and he promptly fell into the candyfloss machine!

BUZZ, SPIN, BUZZ!

Buzby tumbled about in the bowl as the strands of sugar wrapped around him like a cocoon!

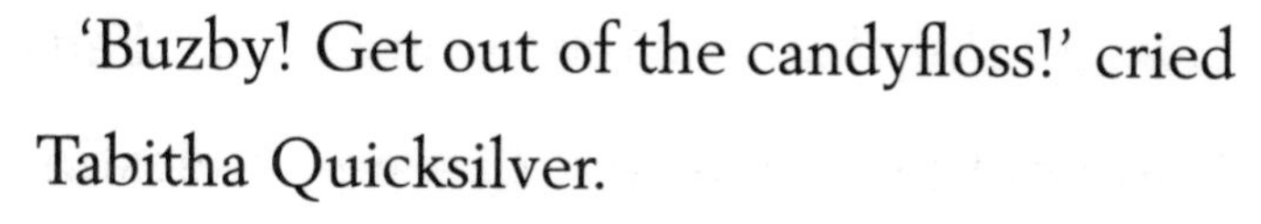

'Buzby! Get out of the candyfloss!' cried Tabitha Quicksilver.

But he couldn't! He was completely stuck . . . and very **dizzy!**

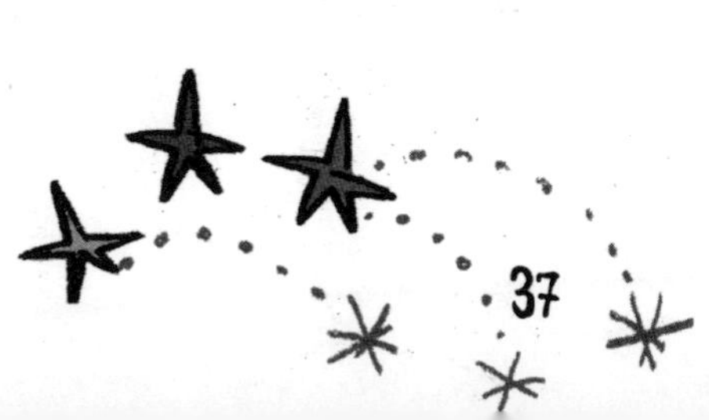

Nixie knew what to do. She looked for the power switch on the machine and flicked it to OFF. The bowl, and Buzby, slowly came to a halt.

'Oh, well done, Nixie,' said the Fairy Queen. 'That *was* quick thinking!'

Nixie blushed and tried to look modest at being praised by *the queen herself!*

But by now poor Buzby looked like a large pink candyfloss—and there was none left in the bowl!

'Um . . . I think I'll give the candyfloss a miss,' said the Fairy Queen, politely.

Buzby's antennae drooped sadly.

Tabitha Quicksilver flicked her magic wand at her little assistant.

TING-a-TING!

A shower of fairy dust instantly turned the sugary mess into a mass of tiny bright pink sparks which fizzed and whooshed up into

the dark night sky like little fireworks!

Nixie and her friends decided waiting for candyfloss would take a very long time, so they headed for the ladybird carousel instead.

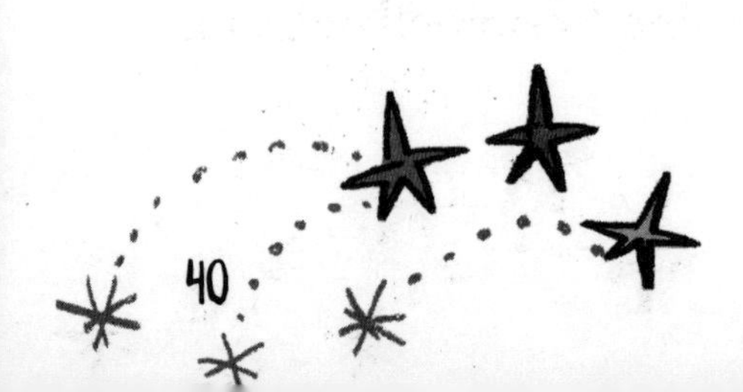

Chapter 5

ADORABELLA LADYBIRD

When they got to the carousel, they stood watching the colourful ladybird cars bobbing up and down as they twirled around the bumpy track. Nixie picked out the car she wanted to go in. It was red with black spots—and just happened to be the one Adorabella was in.

'I bagsy the red one next!' yelled Nixie loudly.

But when the ride stopped, Adorabella refused to get out. She was determined to get her own back on Nixie for picking on her at the dodgems!

'I'm having another go,' she announced smugly.

'That's not fair!' said Nixie.

'You can have that one,' smirked Adorabella, pointing at a pink car with yellow spots.

Nixie's friends were already getting into their ladybird cars.

'Get on, Nixie!' cried Fizz. 'Or the ride will start without you.'

But Nixie didn't want a pink car with yellow spots. She wanted a red car with black spots. So she took her wand out of her boot and pointed it at the pink and yellow car.

It was a very, very bad idea.

Nixie's wonky wand, with its wobbly red star could be very naughty when it wanted to be, which to be honest, was quite often.

Once, to Nixie's horror, it had turned the Fairy Queen's coach into a giant bubble —while the queen was still inside! And then there was the time it had turned Adorabella's dress into a huge snowball— while she was wearing it! And the Fairy Godmother would never forget the time

Nixie's wand had turned her into a huge cupcake with a swirl of butter icing and a cherry on top!

So Nixie probably should have known better than to risk using her mischievous wand, but she decided to do it anyway.

ZAP WHOOSH!

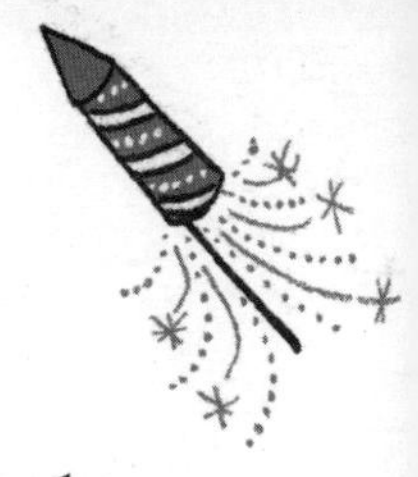

A streak of glittering red fairy dust shot out of her wand like sparks from a firework! And Nixie's naughty wand *deliberately* missed the pink and yellow car—and hit Adorabella instead.

There was a loud GASP!

And a piercing SCREAM!

'Oh no!' cried Nixie.

Adorabella had turned into a ladybird! A red one, with black spots!

'Nixie!' cried Fidget, 'What have you done?'

Nixie was horrified. 'I'm sorry!' she said to Adorabella, 'I didn't mean to do it! It was my wonky wand!' She shook her wand so roughly that the wobbly star nearly fell

off. 'Why are you always so naughty?' she yelled at it crossly. It fizzed back at her cheekily.

'I'm telling the Fairy Godmother,' wailed Adorabella, trying to climb out of the car. But her ladybird bottom was much bigger than her fairy bottom and she was a bit stuck.

'Help! Fairy Godmother! HELP!' she screamed, but Tabitha Quicksilver was at the top of the big wheel with the Fairy Queen and couldn't hear her.

After a bit of a struggle, Adorabella finally managed to clamber out and began to totter about on her spindly ladybird legs. But she wasn't used to having so many legs and she

got them in a tangle, tripped, and tumbled over on to her back. She couldn't get up! As she lay there wailing and **waggling** her legs in the air, Nixie and Fidget rushed to help her while Fizz and Twist darted off to fetch the Fairy Godmother.

Bumblebees' Bottoms, thought Nixie anxiously, *I'm going to be in big, big trouble now.*

Chapter 6

Nixie in the Biggest Trouble . . . Ever!

Nixie couldn't imagine what the Fairy Godmother was going to say. And, even worse, Queen Celestine would be with her!

'What am I going to do?' she gasped.

'You can't do anything!' cried Fidget. 'You'll just have to wait for the Fairy

Godmother to sort it out.'

'You are going to be in the biggest trouble *EVER!*' shrieked Adorabella.

Nixie knew Adorabella was right, *and* that the Fairy Godmother would be there *any minute.*

Just then, a brilliant, but terrible, idea came to her. *If my wonky wand has got me into trouble, then it will just have to get me out of trouble too—by turning Adorabella back into a fairy!*

So she lifted up her wonky wand, steadied the wobbly star, and pointed it at Adorabella.

'Nixie, NO!' cried Fidget.

'Don't you dare use that on me again!' screamed Adorabella.

Nixie ignored them both and . . . **ZAP FIZZLE!**

There was a loud **GASP!**

And a piercing **SCREAM!**

Adorabella hadn't turned back into a fairy—she'd turned into a mushroom! A large red one with black spots! And the Fairy Godmother would be there *any moment*.

'Nooo!' cried Nixie and tried again . . .

ZAP QUACK!

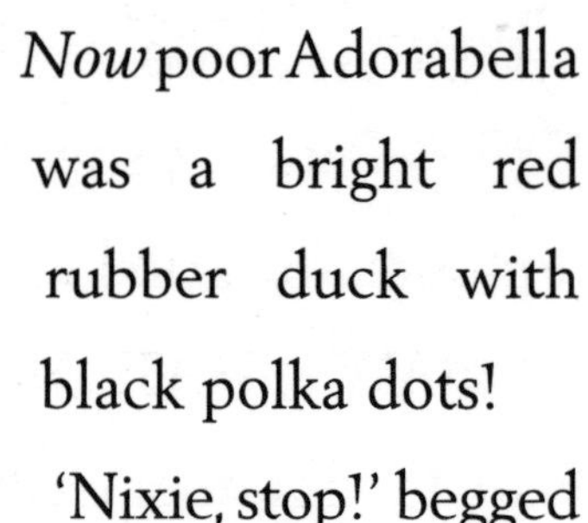

Now poor Adorabella was a bright red rubber duck with black polka dots!

'Nixie, stop!' begged Fidget. 'You're just making it worse!'

'Yes! STOP!' screeched Adorabella.

But Nixie could see the Fairy Godmother fluttering over towards them, closely followed by the Fairy Queen. Frantically she tried one last time . . .

ZAP PLOP!

Adorabella turned into a spotty teapot.

'Bumblebees' bottoms!' wailed Nixie. Quickly, she stuffed her wand into her boot and tried to look all innocent.

'I SAW THAT, NIXIE!' bellowed the Fairy Godmother dashing up. With a quick flick of her wand, Tabitha Quicksilver sprinkled poor Adorabella teapot with a shower of silver fairy dust and **POUFF!** the little fairy was instantly turned back to normal.

'Really Nixie!' fumed Tabitha Quicksilver.

'It was an accident!' stammered Nixie. 'And anyway—she started it!'

'No I didn't!' retorted Adorabella.

'Yes you did—you wouldn't get off the ride!'

'Well that's no excuse to turn poor Adorabella into a teapot!' spluttered the Fairy Godmother.

'But it was my **wonky wand!** I wasn't even aiming at her!' protested Nixie.

'You did it on purpose!' exclaimed Adorabella, wobbling her bottom lip, determined to get Nixie into as much trouble as possible.

'DID NOT!' bawled Nixie.

'YOU BIG FAT HAIRY-FAIRY FIBBER!' yelled Adorabella.

'FAIRIES! Please! Not in front of her Royal Fairy Majesty!' cried Tabitha Quicksilver. The Fairy Queen looked rather shocked.

'Nixie, from now on, keep your wand in your boot. Any more naughtiness from you—or your wand—and you'll go home and miss the fireworks,' said the Fairy Godmother sternly.

'Why do you always think it's my fault?' wailed Nixie.

'Because it nearly always is!' replied Tabitha Quicksilver. 'Oh Nixie, whatever am I going to do with you,' she sighed, and turning to the Fairy Queen added, 'Nixie is just such a . . . well, such a . . .'

'Bad, bad fairy,' finished Adorabella, smugly.

Nixie shot her a filthy look.

Adorabella smirked and stuck out

her tongue at Nixie behind the Fairy Godmother's back. But the Fairy Queen saw and raised an eyebrow at her. Adorabella blushed bubblegum pink.

Chapter 7

I FAIRY DARE YOU!

'Never mind, Nixie,' said Fizz, as the friends fluttered around the funfair. 'It could be worse. You could have been sent home *right now!*'

'But Adorabella's always getting me into trouble with the Fairy Godmother,' moaned Nixie. 'And now even the *Fairy*

Queen thinks it was all my fault!'

Fidget didn't like to point out that actually, rather a lot of it had been Nixie's fault. So instead she said, 'Come on, let's go to the hoopla.'

They all darted over to the stall and Fidget was relieved to see the *Glittery Butterfly Art Kit* prize was still there. The Palace Fairy looking after the stall handed her six wooden hoops.

'You have to throw the hoop right over the prize to win,' he told her.

Eagerly, Fidget hurled her first hoop towards the art kit. A bit too eagerly! She missed—and hit the Palace Fairy on the nose instead!

'Ooops! Sorry!'

'Too hard!' laughed Nixie.

Her second throw was a bit better and actually landed on the table amongst the prizes, but the third hoop hurtled right over the top of them!

Quite by accident, she nearly won a flashing necklace with one throw and then the next hoop finally hit the art kit . . . but bounced off.

'Nooooo!' Fidget squealed in dismay.

'Nearly!' cried Fizz.

Nixie groaned in frustration.

Now Fidget only had one hoop left and Nixie was worried she would miss again.

'Let *me* win it for you,' she said trying to snatch the hoop from her friend. 'I'm a much better thrower than you.'

'No! I want to win it for myself,' said Fidget.

While Nixie and Fidget were busy arguing, Adorabella arrived for a go. The Palace Fairy handed her six hoops.

'Don't you dare aim for the art kit,' Nixie said glaring at Adorabella. 'Fidget's trying to win that.'

'I can if I want to!' announced Adorabella and so, just to annoy Nixie, she deliberately aimed for the art kit. Scowling with concentration she threw her first hoop and it sailed through the air towards the prizes.

Fidget and her friends held their breath in horror as, by sheer good luck, the wooden ring landed neatly over the art set with a soft clatter.

Fidget burst into tears.

'You did that on purpose!' snapped Nixie. 'Give me the art set,' she demanded, with her hand out, 'I'll win you something else.'

'No!' retorted Adorabella, putting her prize behind her back.

'Oh, please,' begged Twist.

'Fidget really, really wants it,' added Fizz.

'No! I won it!' cried Adorabella.

Nixie's green eyes glittered with anger. 'Hand it over . . . or else.'

'Or else what?' said Adorabella.

'I'll turn you into a slug.'

A sneaky look crept across Adorabella's face. Of course, she didn't actually want to be turned into a slug, but she knew that if Nixie did something as naughty as that then the Fairy Godmother would send her straight home. So she crossed her arms, looked Nixie right in eye and said, 'Go on then, turn me into a slug. I fairy dare you!'

Nixie's friends gasped. Nixie never ever turned down a dare. To their dismay she

reached for her wand . . .

'NO!' cried Twist.

'Nixie, DON'T!' begged Fizz.

'She's just trying to get you into trouble,' warned Fidget.

Nixie clenched her fists and glared at Adorabella . . . who smirked back. Nixie's fingers itched to snatch up her wand.

'You'll be sent home!' Fidget pointed out urgently.

Nixie seethed and her face went redder than her dress—but she knew she had to back down. Adorabella flounced off, smiling, taking the art kit with her.

Nixie was furious, but Twist turned to her and said in a voice that was little more

than a whisper, 'It is partly your fault too, Nixie.'

'How?' demanded Nixie, going all hot in the face.

'Well, if we'd come over to the hoopla when Fidget wanted to, then she could have had more goes and she might have won the art kit,' said Twist.

'That's not fair!' retorted Nixie.

'Yes it is,' said Fizz. 'You've been a bossy britches all night, Nixie, making us all do what *you* wanted to do.'

'No I haven't, have I, Fidget?' demanded Nixie, hoping her friend would back her up. But Fidget just bit her lip and nobody said anything.

Nixie's eyes went all stingy and she turned away. Then, tensing her little black wings she darted off—on her own.

'Nixie! Come back!' cried the others. But she didn't.

Chapter 8

A LOUD CLUNK AND A HUGE JOLT!

Adorabella had fluttered over to have a go on the big wheel. But there was nobody there! The Palace Fairy meant to be looking after the ride had nipped off to get some candyfloss. Funnily enough, he'd been gone quite a long time!

Adorabella gazed longingly at the

massive wheel. Its coloured lights flashed invitingly. *A whole fairground ride, all to myself!* she thought. It was too good a chance to miss—even if she would have to use a little magic to get it going! Of course the fairies weren't allowed to waste magic—the Fairy Godmother was pretty strict about that—so Adorabella looked round to make sure no one was watching, then she hurriedly jumped into a seat, slamming the little door of the carriage behind her. She pointed her sparkly yellow wand at the start button on the machine and **TING!** A stream of yellow fairy dust struck the button and set the big wheel turning—all on its own.

CREAK! WHIRR!

Smiling smugly, she settled back to enjoy the ride. UP and UP and UP she rose . . . until she could see the whole of the fairground and the Enchanted Palace beneath her. It was fabulous!

But suddenly, there was a loud

CLUNK!

And a huge

JOLT!

And the big wheel shuddered to a stop!

'What's happened?' cried Adorabella, looking down to see if someone had stopped the ride. But nobody had. She picked up her wand and aimed it at the

start button again. She was a long way up so she had to give it a good hard flick . . .

Ooooops!

Her wand flew out of her hand. She watched in alarm as it tumbled all the way down to the ground below.

'Oh no!' she cried, and she tried to open the door of the carriage to fly down and get it. But in her rush to get in, she'd caught her dress in the door and it was jammed shut! She was stuck—right at the top of the big wheel.

'Help!' she screamed. 'HELP!'

Meanwhile, Nixie was wandering aimlessly around the fair all on her own, wishing she hadn't fallen out with her friends.

It's no fun at all being on your own at a funfair, she thought, kicking at the grass with her great clompy boots. And then she remembered poor Twist sitting all alone while they'd all gone on the spinning teacups without her, and how Fidget had said she'd go on the hoopla stall with her instead. Actually, now that she came to think about it *perhaps* it might *possibly* have been *partly* her fault that Fidget hadn't won the art set after all. She sighed miserably.

Suddenly she heard a voice yelling.

'HELP! SOMEBODY HELP!'

It was coming from the big wheel, so she darted over and, looking up, saw Adorabella

all on her own, right at the top. She also saw, underneath the wheel, Adorabella's sparkly yellow wand. She pounced on it gleefully!

'Hey, Adorabella! I've got your wand!' she yelled up, her eyes sparkling with mischief.

'Give it back!' bawled Adorabella.

'Come and get it!'

'I can't!'

'Why not?'

'Because the big wheel's stuck . . . the door's stuck . . . and I'm stuck!' wailed Adorabella.

Nixie roared with laughter.

'It's not funny!' screeched Adorabella. 'Go and get the Fairy Godmother!'

Nixie had a quick look around, but the Fairy Godmother was nowhere in sight.

Chapter 9

Nixie's Trusty Spanner

It *would serve Adorabella right if she was stuck on the big wheel all night!* thought Nixie. But then nobody else would be able to go on the ride either, she realized, and she hadn't even had a go yet.

So she called up to Adorabella, 'Hang on, and I'll fix the ride and get you down.'

'Don't you **dare** use your wonky wand!' screeched Adorabella. 'It'll do something horrible to me, like turning the big wheel into a giant spinning top . . . or a Catherine wheel!'

Nixie grinned wickedly. The idea of sending Adorabella spinning round and round super fast in a fizzing Catherine wheel was very tempting! But she knew the Fairy Godmother would definitely send her home if she did that.

So she yelled up, 'I don't need **magic** to mend a machine!'

But she *did* need both hands, so she stuffed Adorabella's wand down her boot next to her trusty spanner.

As she looked up, she saw Fizz darting towards her. 'Nixie! We've been looking for you everywhere!'

'Have you? But I thought everyone was cross with me?' said Nixie.

'Don't be daft!' grinned Fizz. 'We're always friends—always.'

Nixie beamed at him. 'Well in that case, can you go and find the Fairy Godmother? Adorabella's stuck on the big wheel and it's broken down!'

'Of course,' said Fizz, and he darted off.

In the meantime, Nixie opened up the cover of the big wheel's engine. The first thing she did was turn the machine to OFF, and then she had a good look inside. Nixie always says you can often see why a machine has stopped working—which makes it easier to work out how to mend it. She soon saw the problem. One of the big bolts had wobbled loose and fallen off. So she grabbed her trusty spanner, rattled the bolt back into place, and tightened it up.

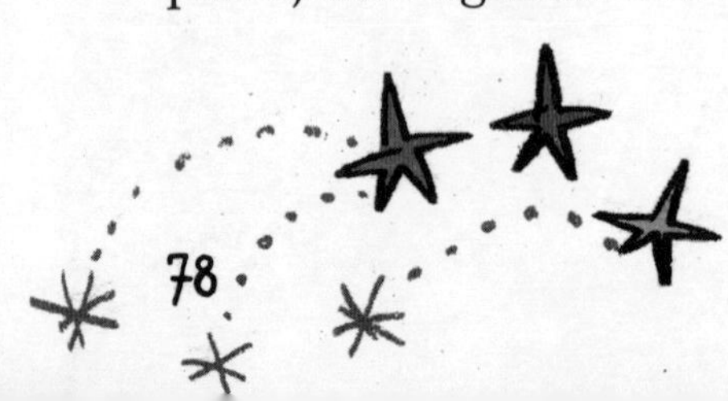

'All fixed!' she called up to Adorabella.

'Well don't just stand there! Get me down!' screeched Adorabella.

'Ask nicely,' said Nixie.

'NO!' snapped Adorabella. She looked around to see if the Fairy Godmother was on her way, but she couldn't see her anywhere.

'GET ME DOWN!' she bellowed to Nixie.

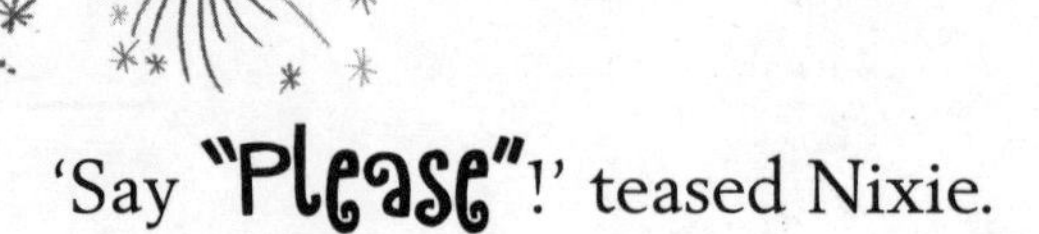

'Say **"Please"**!' teased Nixie.

Adorabella glared down at her. 'Please,' she snapped.

'Now say **"Sorry"** for being a horrible meany at the hoopla stall,' said Nixie, beginning to enjoy herself.

'I wasn't a horrible meany at the hoopla!' protested Adorabella.

'Yes you were! You went and won the prize Fidget wanted,' snapped Nixie heatedly.

'It was only a silly art set!' said Adorabella.

'But you knew that Fidget wanted it and you did it on purpose!' cried Nixie angrily.

'Fine! She can have it!' flounced Adorabella and, much to Nixie's surprise,

she threw the *Glitter Butterfly Art Kit* down to her!

'Oh! Thank you!' cried Nixie darting up to catch it. She hadn't expected Adorabella to do that!

Nixie turned the big wheel machine back on and pressed the start button.

CLUNK! WHIRR! CREAK!

The wheel slowly started to turn, bringing Adorabella slowly down to the ground.

It was just at this moment that Fizz rushed back, with the Fairy Godmother and Queen Celestine in tow.

'Fizz says that poor Adorabella's stuck at the top of the big wheel!' panted the Fairy Godmother anxiously.

'She was, but I managed to mend the engine and rescue her,' said Nixie modestly. She put the cover back over the engine, slid her spanner into her boot, and wiped her hands on her grubby red dress.

'Nixie! I'm very impressed!' said Queen Celestine, smiling at her, and then, turning to Adorabella she added, 'Come and say "Thank you" to Nixie.'

But the carriage door was still jammed shut so Adorabella couldn't get out. The Fairy Godmother fixed it with a flick of her wand and Adorabella fluttered over. She was still determined to get Nixie into trouble, so instead of thanking her, she burst into fake tears!

'Nixie's got my wand and she won't give it back!' she sobbed.

Nixie looked down and gasped—Adorabella's sparkly yellow wand was still in her boot!

'NIXIE! That's very naughty! Give it back *immediately!*' spluttered the Fairy Godmother.

Speechless, Nixie thrust the wand at Adorabella.

'Nixie, you will go home—*right now* and miss the fireworks,' announced the Fairy Godmother furiously.

'But . . . but . . .' stammered Nixie.

Chapter 10

Missing Earmuffs

The Fairy Queen raised her hand regally. 'Actually, I don't think Nixie *should* be sent home,' she said.

The Fairy Godmother's eyebrows rose in surprise.

'Well, she *did* keep her wand in her boot, and she *didn't* use any magic. So in fact

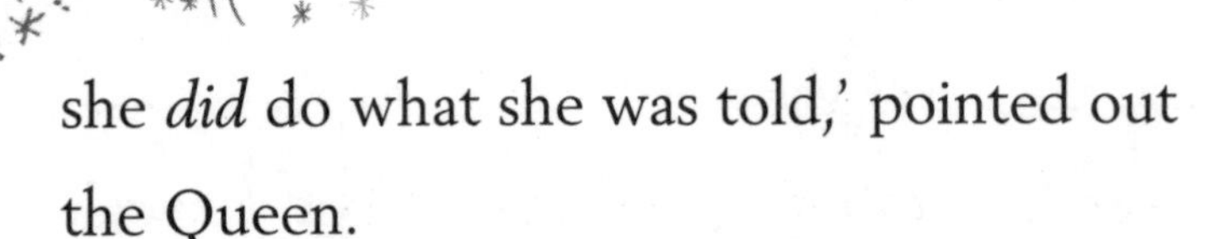

she *did* do what she was told,' pointed out the Queen.

'But she also took Adorabella's wand, and that was naughty,' replied Tabitha Quicksilver.

'Well, perhaps a *bit* naughty. But, on the other hand, she was *extremely* good to rescue Adorabella,' said the Queen, smiling at Nixie. 'And anyhow, it's already time for the **fireworks.**' And with that she took Tabitha Quicksilver off with her to sort out the display.

Nixie shot Adorabella a look—she was so going to get her back for that!

'Come on, let's find the others,' said Fizz. So Nixie tucked the art kit under her arm,

and together they flitted off. As they flew over the toffee apple stall Nixie darted down. 'I just need to get one of these for Twist!' she said.

'I want one too!' laughed Fizz.

In the end they got four of the **scrummy gooey apples** and set off again to look for their friends. They eventually found them with the other fairies, waiting for the fireworks.

Tabitha Quicksilver and the Fairy Queen had set up the fireworks in front of the Enchanted Palace and now all the fairies were clustered eagerly along a rope barrier the Palace Fairies had strung up for safety. Buzby was making sure everyone was

staying behind it.

Fizz gave out the toffee apples and Nixie proudly handed over the *Glittery Butterfly Art Kit* to Fidget, who flung her arms round her in a big hug.

'Thank you! But how did you get it?' she cried.

'Adorabella just sort of gave it to me,' shrugged Nixie. *Well, that's nearly true,* she thought. 'I'm sorry for being bossy,' she added, 'and specially for making you sit out on your own, Twist.'

'That's all right,' mumbled Twist with her mouth full of toffee apple.

Nixie grinned at her.

Then she clutched Fidget excitedly and squealed in her ear, **'Ooooh!** I can't wait for the fireworks!'

Fidget gasped! 'Where are my earmuffs?' she cried. She'd lost them!

'What am I going to do? I HATE the

sound of fireworks. They're too loud and they make me jump.'

'Don't worry, we'll find your earmuffs,' said Nixie and they all dashed off to search the fairground. They went back to every single place Fidget had been that night, but they couldn't see them anywhere.

'I'll have to go home,' announced Fidget sadly.

'But you can't!' cried Nixie.

'Don't start being bossy again!' said Twist.

'I'm not! It's just that it's horrible being on your own when everyone else is having fun.'

But by now all the fairies were counting down to the start of the firework display.

'Ten . . . nine . . .' they yelled.

Fidget sighed and turned to flutter off home.

'WAIT!' cried Nixie. 'I've got an idea!'

'Eight!'

She grabbed Twist's hairband.

'Seven!'

And swiped Fizz's mittens!

'Six!'

She asked a Water Fairy who was standing nearby, for a handful of candyfloss.

'Five!'

Then she grasped her wonky wand firmly, begged it to behave itself, and . . . ZAP TING! She turned the candyfloss into cotton wool.

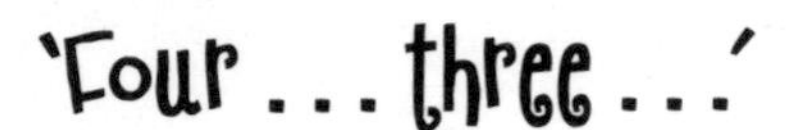

yelled the rest of the fairies gleefully as Nixie stuffed the cotton wool into the mittens and shoved the ends of Twist's plastic hairband firmly down into the middle of each one. Before you could say 'wonky wands' she'd made Fidget a pair of fluffy earmuffs!

'Two . . .'

She crammed them onto Fidget's head . . . just in time!

'ONE!' finished the fairies excitedly.

Suddenly . . .

WHEEEEEEE!

An enormous rocket whoooshed up into the dark sky and exploded.

BANG!

Everyone jumped and screamed—except Fidget. Nixie's mitten earmuffs worked brilliantly!

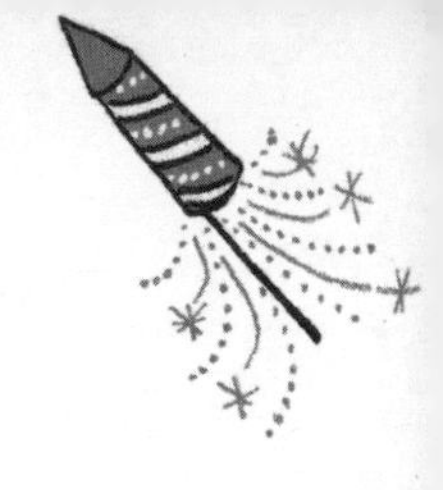

Chapter 11

FABULOUS FIREWORKS FUN!

The Fairy Queen was busy lighting the fireworks—with magic! Her beautiful sparkly wand sent streams of silvery fairy dust to spark the fuses, one after another. High above the Enchanted Palace rockets screamed across the sky and burst into billowing cascades of red and silver sparks.

WHEEE . . . KABOOM!

'Yahoooo!' yelled Nixie. Lots of the fairies squealed and grabbed each other. The noise was so loud that poor Bubzy jumped and tumbled over backwards in mid-air!

WHOOSH . . . WHOOSH . . . SPARKLE!

'Oooooh!' gasped the fairies, as dozens of fizzing fireworks whizzed upwards, trailing

spirals of silver sparks behind them.

'Aaaaah!' sighed everyone as

FIZZZZ!

SPARKLE!

SPARKLE!

An entire row of roman candles gushed up into fountains of brightly coloured sparks.

'They're sooo lovely!' exclaimed Twist, her eyes shining.

'I love the pretty coloured ones most!' yelled Fidget extremely loudly. She was shouting because she was deafened by her mitten earmuffs!

Nixie grinned and gazed skywards, her excited face lit by the glow of the fireworks.

Then

BANG-A-BANG! SNAP-A-SNAP!

Hundreds of deafening firecrackers rattled and spluttered explosively on the grass in front of them!

Fizz whooped. 'The noisy ones are best!' he yelled at Nixie.

'They're brilliant!' she hollered back.

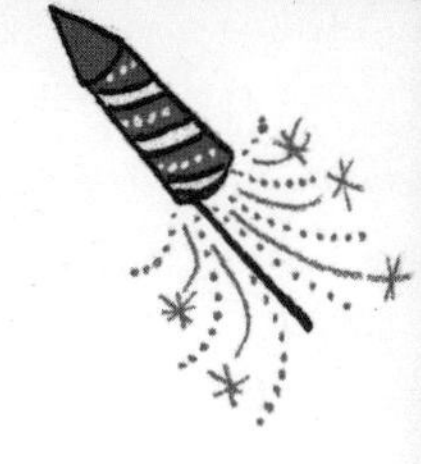

Just then, there was the most enormous

KA-BOOM!

And everybody jumped as a gigantic rocket exploded just above them, sending dozens of sparkling fireballs fizzing across the sky in every direction until

KA-KA-KA-BOOM!

All the little fireballs burst into cascading clusters of blue and red sparks.

Adorabella screamed and grabbed hold of the Fairy Godmother.

Nixie screamed at the top of her voice too. Actually she wasn't scared *at all.* She just thinks screaming at the top of her voice is all part of the fun at a fireworks display!

Finally, a huge fizzing rocket roared way, way up into the dark sky. They all watched it climb higher and higher. Then there was a pause as it seemed to hang in mid-air, and then

BOOM!

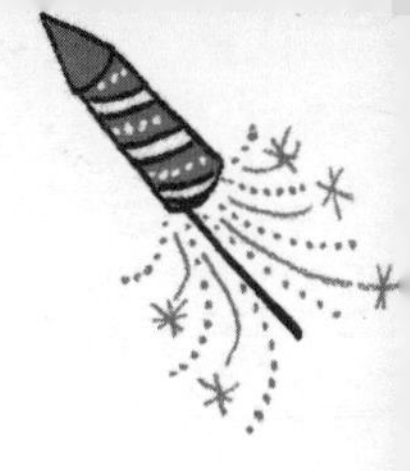

It was biggest blast ever!

Twist **squealed** and clutched on to Fidget, and even Nixie **squeaked** with shock.

'That scared me!' laughed Fizz.

Then, suddenly, it was quiet. The bitter smell of smoke drifted above everyone, leaving coloured trails floating in the night air. The fairies wondered sadly if that was the end.

But then the Fairy Queen beckoned to Nixie.

Nixie gulped and exchanged a worried look with Fizz.

Bumblebees' bottoms! She thought anxiously, *what have I done wrong now?*

Chapter 12

FIZZING WHIZZING DOUGHNUTS!

But Nixie needn't have worried—she wasn't in trouble at all. Queen Celestine had been so impressed when Nixie rescued Adorabella and fixed the big wheel (with a spanner instead of magic), that she had decided Nixie deserved a treat. She was going to let her light the fuse for the

spectacular firework finale.

The whole of the front of the Enchanted Palace was covered with fireworks. There were thousands of tiny sparklers stuck round the windows and doors, dozens of rainbow fountains perched on the roof and turrets, and hundreds of Catherine wheels pinned all along the walls. They would all be set off by one big fuse, and Nixie was going to light it —with her wand!

She was beside herself with pride as she stood next to Queen Celestine. All her friends cheered, and Adorabella scowled at her jealously.

The Fairy Godmother was terribly anxious. She couldn't believe the Queen was going

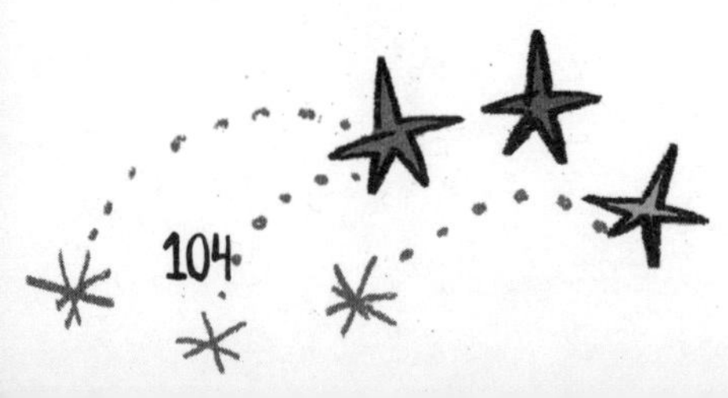

to let Nixie, and her wonky wand, anywhere near a pile of fireworks! She clutched her own wand nervously and stood by—in case of an emergency.

Of course, Queen Celestine knew it was probably bit risky, but it wasn't Nixie's fault that her wand was so naughty and she thought Nixie should have a chance.

Nervously, Nixie took her wonky wand out of her boot, steadied the wobbly star, and pointed it at the big blue paper fuse.

'Don't you dare show me up in front of the Fairy Queen herself,' she hissed at it sternly. She was absolutely dreading what her naughty wand might do next. She could only hope it had had enough mischief for one day.

It hadn't.

Nixie aimed directly at the fuse, but her wand wobbled wildly and **ZAP-a-ZAP** sent a stream of hot bright red sparks heading straight for the Catherine wheels stuck on the wall!

FIZZ WHIZZ!

The Catherine wheels all spluttered and started spinning round furiously!

'Bumblebees' Bottoms!' squealed Nixie. But, as she looked on nervously, she saw that the Catherine wheels weren't Catherine wheels any more. Her cheeky wand had turned them into iced doughnuts—all covered in hundreds and thousands! They were all whooshing round like crazy,

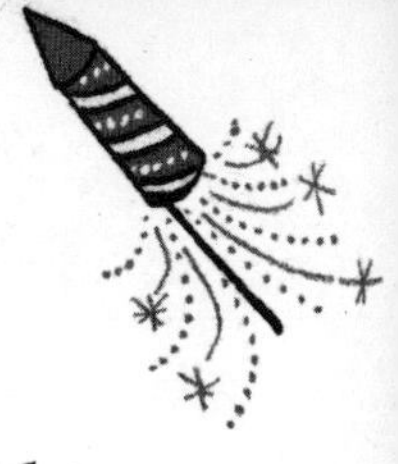

showering everyone with sugar sprinkles!

And then—to Nixie's horror,

ZOOM ZOOM WHOOOSH!

The doughnuts whirled right off the walls and straight at the fairies!

'Nixie! What have you done?' cried the Fairy Godmother, ducking as a doughnut sailed just over her head.

FIZZ SPLUTTER FIZZ!

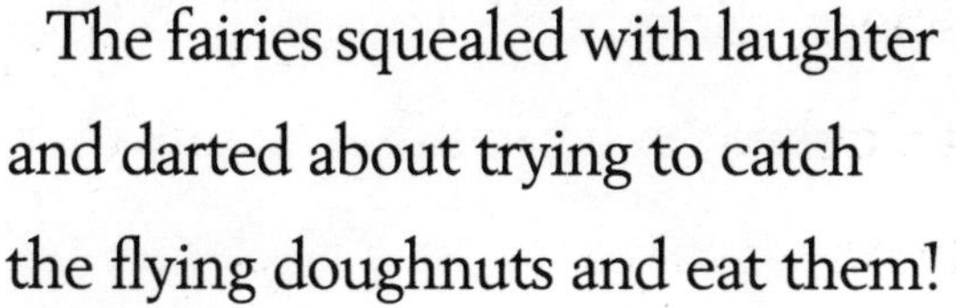

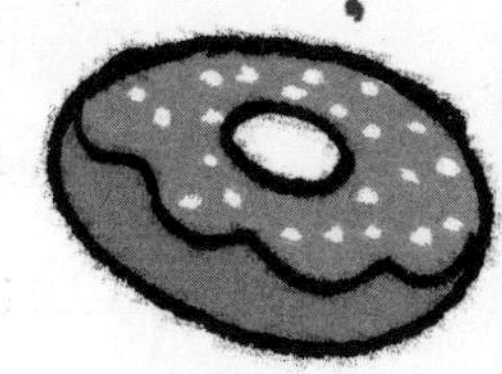

The fairies squealed with laughter and darted about trying to catch the flying doughnuts and eat them!

'Never mind, Nixie,' laughed Queen Celestine, 'I love doughnuts!' Deftly she caught a doughnut in one hand, and lit the firework fuse with her wand in the other one!

There was a

WHOOOSH

And a

FIZZ

And then everyone

GASPED!

The whole of the front of the Enchanted Palace erupted into a dazzling display of glittering fireworks. It looked even more magical than ever!

Nixie busily zipped around grabbing a handful of doughnuts. Then, to serve her wand right for being naughty, she turned it upside down and used the wonky handle as a doughnut holder!

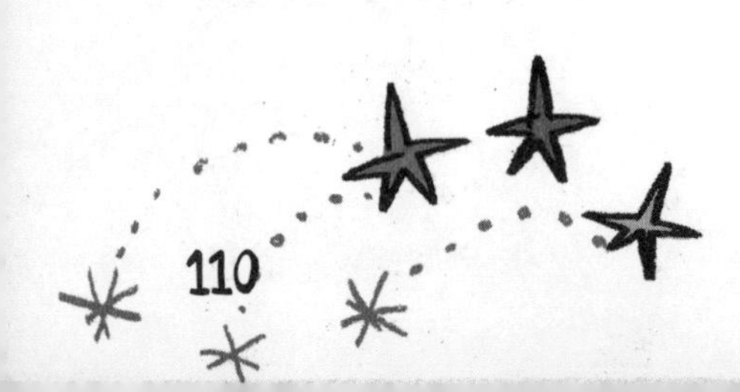

Chapter 13

ADORASMELLA IS A STINKYPOO

The fairies happily munched doughnuts and watched the fizzing fireworks light up the entire Enchanted Palace. Soon it was all over though, and the last spark had fizzled out. But the fun didn't end there!

The Fairy Godmother told everyone to

put on their gloves. Fidget handed Fizz his mittens back and he shook the cotton wool out of them and hurriedly pulled them on. Then, when all the fairies were wearing their gloves, the Fairy Queen told them to hold up their wands and, with a smattering of silver fairy dust, she turned all their wands into fizzing sparklers!

'Oooooh!' cried the fairies! Laughing and giggling and darting round the dark sky, they wrote their names and made crazy zigzag shapes with their wands. The patterns glowed and hung in

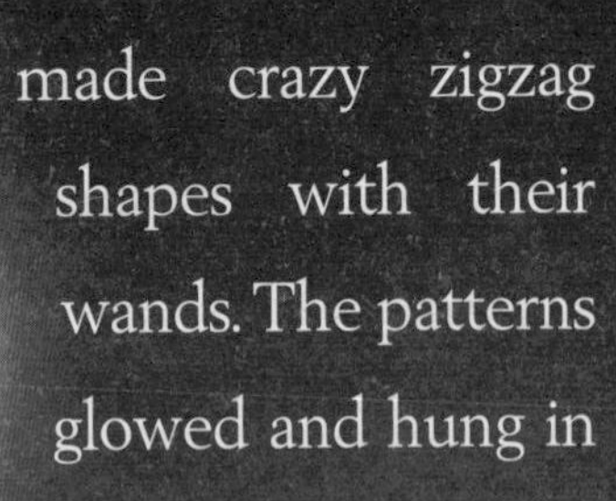

the air for ages. Fizz and Fidget even managed to play a game of noughts and crosses before the lines faded.

Nixie tried writing and making shapes with her wonky wand, but it was too wobbly. So she gave up trying to use her wand as a sparkler and instead set her mind to thinking about how to get Adorabella back for telling lies and getting her into trouble with the Fairy Godmother. Funnily enough, it was her naughty wand that gave her a marvellously mischievous idea!

Looking about to make sure no one was watching, she pointed her wand at Adorabella's and gave it a small, sneaky flick! ZAP! Perhaps it was because Nixie's plan was brilliantly bad, but this time Nixie's wand decided to do exactly what Nixie wanted.

Nixie enchanted Adorabella's wand so that instead of writing what Adorabella wanted it to write, it wrote what Nixie wanted it to write—in great big letters! And Adorabella couldn't stop it!

'Adorasmella is a stinkypoo' wrote Adorabella's wand, much to her surprise and dismay. Then it added, 'The Fairy Godmother is a Fairy Pong-mother' and

'Queen Celestine is the Hairy Queen'!

Adorabella gasped, utterly horrified, but everyone else shrieked with laughter. Except the Fairy Godmother, who was livid!

'Adorabella! Stop that at once!' she exclaimed.

But of course, Adorabella couldn't.

'Buzby is a Bum Bum Bee' wrote her wand.

'Stop writing such rude things!' snapped Tabitha Quicksilver.

'It's not me! It's my wand!' wailed Adorabella.

'Oh for goodness' sake!' replied the Fairy Godmother, rolling her eyes. 'We all know Nixie's wonky wand is naughty and doesn't always do what she tells it to, but yours is not and you don't have that excuse!'

Behind the Fairy Godmother's back, the Queen was trying to keep a straight face. Then, calmly and secretly, she aimed her own wand at Adorabella's and TING! suddenly, Adorabella's wand stopped writing.

The Fairy Queen turned to Adorabella

and exclaimed in a loud and shocked voice, 'Adorabella! I can't imagine what got into you tonight!'

Poor Adorabella gasped and blushed bright pink.

Then the Queen turned to Nixie and gave her a big wink! Nixie grinned and gave her a cheeky wink back!

Acknowledgements

Nixie the Bad, Bad Fairy says:

Zoom . . . whoosh . . . BOOM! 'Thank you Kathy Webb and Gill Sore at OUP for all your **fabulous** help and making sure I had so much Fizzy Firework Fun!'

Fizzle, whizz, sparkle, sparkle . . . WHEEEE! 'Huge thanks to the lovely Ali Pye! Your **amazing** illustrations make me look brilliant!'

Crackle, fizz, and BANG-A-BANG! 'Thank you both, Sarah Darby and Lizzie Smart, for making all the pages in all my Nixie books so **dazzling!**'

Whoosh . . . screech . . . ZOOM! '**Massive** thanks to that wonderful Gaia Banks for applying rockets to that Cas Lester and making her invent me in the first place!'

And . . . whoosh, whizz, and KA-KA-KA-BOOM! 'Bestest thanks of all to Cas Lester's children for being soooo full of **mischief**—especially that Annie Beth, the *original* Bad, Bad Fairy. **Bumblebees' Bottoms** you lot have been a tough act to follow!'

Cas Lester says:

'Nixie! Get off my computer!'

About the illustrator

I have wanted to illustrate books for almost as long as I can remember. When I was little I spent lots of time drawing and thinking up stories. I often got told off for 'having my nose in a book' or doodling when I was supposed to be helping my family—now I have to nag my own children for exactly the same reasons!

About the author

I used to make children's television programmes for CBBC like *Jackanory* and *The Story of Tracy Beaker.* But now I'm writing books for children instead, which is great because it means I can spend much more time mucking about with my family and with Bramble, my daft dog. And I get to do lots of school visits, which I absolutely love. I'm also the author of the Harvey Drew books—comedy adventures set in outer space.

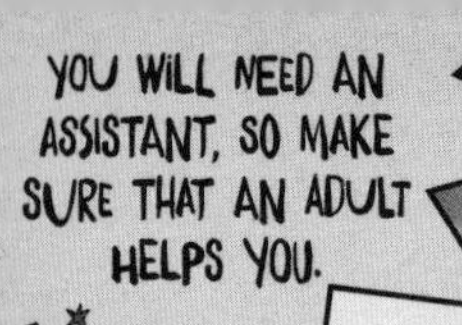

Tabitha Quicksilver's Catherine Wheel Cookies

Sweet, swirly,
and coated in sprinkles!

MESSY FUN!

YOU WILL NEED:

- 150G CASTER SUGAR
- 175G SOFTENED BUTTER
- 2TSP VANILLA EXTRACT
- 1 EGG
- 300G PLAIN FLOUR, PLUS EXTRA FOR DUSTING
- COLOURFUL SPRINKLES
- 200G ICING SUGAR
- 2-3TBSP WATER

1 Preheat the oven to 180°C/160°C fan oven/gas 4.

2 Start your dough by beating together caster sugar and butter with a wooden spoon until the mixture goes smooth. Then mix in the vanilla extract and egg.

3 Sift in the flour, and use the wooden spoon to bring the dough together into one big lump.

4 On a lightly floured surface, use a rolling pin to roll the dough to 1cm thickness. And then use a cookie cutter or upturned glass to press out your circle shape.

5 Next, place your biscuits onto a lined and greased baking tray and pop into the oven. Bake them for 10 minutes, then leave to cool on a wire rack.

6 When your biscuits are cooled, it's time for the fun part, decorating! First, mix your water and icing sugar in a bowl to create a runny icing mixture.

7 Dip a teaspoon into the icing and use it to drizzle a swirly pattern onto each biscuit.

8 Finish with a sprinkling of sprinkles—then they're ready to eat. YUM!

YOU WILL NEED AN ASSISTANT, SO MAKE SURE THAT AN ADULT HELPS YOU.

Nixie's Homemade Hoopla

Create your own fairground stall with these simple instructions.

YOU WILL NEED:

- 8 PAPER PLATES
- 5 CARDBOARD TOILET ROLL TUBES
- PAINT OR COLOURED PENS TO DECORATE YOUR PLATES
- SCISSORS

1 Start by decorating the edges of three paper plates, these will be your hoops. **Top tip:** Look through the illustrations in the book for pattern and design ideas.

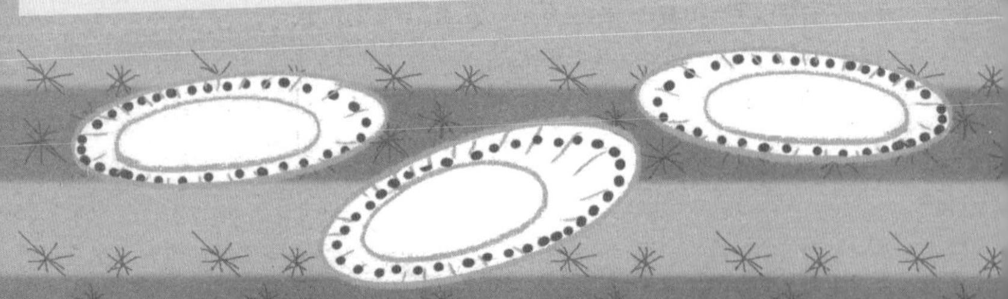

2 Cut the middle out of your three plates to create hoops.

3 Take the other five paper plates, turn them upside down, and label the edge of each plate from 1 to 5.

4 Next, cut a 5 cm cross into the centre of each plate, and push the cardboard tube through to hold it in place. Your paper plate should act as a stand to keep the tube in place as you play.

5 Position each cardboard tube at different distances away from you, with 1 the closest, and 5 the furthest away. Then you're ready to play!

6 The game works like this: each player gets three goes to try and throw a hoop over a cardboard tube. The number on each plate is the score you get if your hoop lands over the tube. Once your turn is up, add the three scores together. The player with the highest score wins!

Collect them all!

The Bad, Bad Fairy

Bumblebees' Bottoms! Nixie the Bad, Bad Fairy is in BIG trouble when her wand goes missing on the day of the Blossom Ball. She'll have to think up one of her clever plans to get out of this mess!

Wonky Winter Wonderland

Snow days are for sledging, skating and snowball battles and no one is safe from Nixie's expertly aimed snowballs or her mischievous wonky wand. But one fairy is missing out on all of the fun: where is Fidget the butterfly fairy? It's up to Nixie to find her and prove that she's not such a bad, bad fairy but a rather ingenious one!

Splashy Summer Swim

When it's a super hot sunny day, there's only one thing to do with all your friends . . . have a WATER FIGHT! For Nixie the naughty fairy this is the perfect opportunity to come up with some of her ingenious inventions to make the fairies' swimming party really go with a splash . . . and a BANG! Oops! Her wonky wand is up to its usual tricks and soon the peaceful pond becomes a froggy fiasco!

Fizzy Firework Fun

It's the night of the Fairyland Funfair and Nixie the Bad, Bad Fairy can't wait to go on all of her favourite rides! To top it all off there will be a HUGE fizzy firework display to close the fair. Buzzing with excitement, thrill-seeker Nixie rushes from one ride to the next; but Nixie's impatient nature and wonky wand soon get her into trouble!

Love Nixie? Then we know you're going to enjoy reading about these fantastic characters too . . .